AT THE WATERHOLE

BETH SHOSHAN

ILLUSTRATED BY

PIERS HARPER

meadowside

HOP,
swoop,
fly,
soar,

flicker, flutter, flurry...

CRASH! BANG!
CLATTER!
BOOM!

whoosh!
swish, scurry!

Roar! Growl!
Bellow! Bawl!
Snip!
Crack!
Snap!

crash! BOOM!

hoosh, SWish,

flitter, flutter, flap.

stomp! stamp!
Stumble! plod!
Drift, float, glide...

growl!
snap!
Bang! BOOM!
whoosh!
swoop, slide...

grunt, growl, grumble, moan.

Scuttle, scurry, dash!

stomp, stamp!
Glide,
growl!
snap!
Bang!
crash

Slink, Slither,
squirm, slide...
screeech,
cackle,
WHOOP!

Growl
Scurry,
Plod!
Roar!
Bang!
swish,

whizz, zoom,

race, rush! sleepy, sluggish, slooww.

Slither,
whoop!
screeech!

THUD!
Bang!
CRASH!
NOOOOOO!!

Wallop, wham, thump, bump, stomp, stamp, Smash!

Crunch, crack, thudder, thwack,

splish, splosh...

SPL

aSH!